Walking the Dragon's Back

By M.M. Eboch

Illustrated by Sarah Horne

Rourke
Educational Media
rourkeeducationalmedia.com

www.rourkeeducationalmedia.com

Edited by: Keli Sipperley
Cover and Interior layout by: Renee Brady
Cover and Interior Illustrations by: Sarah Horne

Library of Congress PCN Data

Walking the Dragon's Back / M.M. Eboch
(Rourke's World Adventure Chapter Books)
ISBN (hard cover)(alk. paper) 978-1-63430-396-5
ISBN (soft cover) 978-1-63430-496-2
ISBN (e-Book) 978-1-63430-590-7
Library of Congress Control Number: 2015933791

Printed in the United States of America, North Mankato, Minnesota

Dear Parents and Teachers:

Rourke's Adventure Chapter Books engage readers immediately by grabbing their attention with exciting plots and adventurous characters.

Our Adventure Chapter Books offer longer, more complex sentences and chapters. With minimal illustrations, readers must rely on the descriptive text to understand the setting, characters, and plot of the book. Each book contains several detailed episodes all centered on a single plot that will challenge the reader.

Each adventure book dives into a country. Readers are not only invited to tag along for the adventure but will encounter the most memorable monuments and places, culture, and history. As the characters venture throughout the country, they address topics of family, friendship, and growing up in a way that the reader can relate to.

Whether readers are reading the books independently or you are reading with them, engaging with them after they have read the book is still important. We've included several activities at the end of each book to make this both fun and educational.

Are you ready for this adventure?

Enjoy,
Rourke Educational Media

Table of Contents

The Forbidden City............................ 6

Alone in a Crowd 17

The Dragon's Back............................25

Buried Ghosts 34

Mirrors in the Sky............................45

What's in the Wall?..........................56

Meeting a Mongol............................ 66

Sounds in the Night..........................72

Thieves!...................................... 82

Chapter One

The Forbidden City

"The Forbidden City!" Jaden said.

Grace crossed the hotel room to see what her brother was holding.

"What are you talking about?"

"It's one of the places on this card. You mark where you want to go and show it to the taxi driver if he doesn't speak English. The Forbidden City. Doesn't it sound cool?" Jaden grinned.

"Right, I saw something about that." Grace picked up the China guidebook from the desk and flipped a few pages. "It's number one on the top experiences list for China. It says it's a big palace. Lots of history. Mom would like that." Their mother was a history professor at a university in Seattle. But she wasn't with them on this trip. She and Dad would be returning in a month to pick up their new adopted sister. On this visit, it was only

Dad, Grace, and Jaden.

"It says the palace has legend and intrigue too," Grace added.

"Intrigue is like mystery, right?" Jaden asked, leaning over her shoulder. "And it says it's easy to get lost!"

Getting lost was Jaden's favorite pastime.

"No getting lost in China, please!" Their dad called out from another room in the hotel suite. He came into their room. "Seriously, kids. We'll have plenty of excitement while hiking the Great Wall. But first, are you ready to go to the orphanage?"

"I still say, if we have to get another kid, we should get a boy," Jaden grumbled.

Dad ruffled his hair. "Maybe next time, if there is a next time."

"One brother is enough," Grace said. "In fact, it's one too many." Jaden stuck out his tongue at her.

"Remember, we're just going to an orphanage here in Beijing to drop off some presents," Dad said. "We won't be meeting your new sister yet."

"I don't understand why we can't," Grace said.

"I don't really either," Dad said. "But adopting

a child takes a long time, and there are many rules to follow." He kissed the top of Grace's head. "This visit is so you can see where you came from, and Jaden can see where his sisters are from."

"And so you can write your article," Grace said. Dad grinned.

"I always enjoy mixing business and pleasure," he said.

Dad wrote about travel and food for magazines. He often turned their vacations into research trips for his articles.

Grace looked out the window while Jaden tried to find his shoes. The city seemed endless, packed full of buildings and cars and bicycles and people. It was spread out on a flat plain, with mountains in the distance. The day before they had spent 11 hours on an airplane, flying from Seattle in America to Beijing, China.

For the first time since she was a baby, Grace was back in the country where she was born. Her American parents adopted her when she was eight months old. They were white. Her eight-year-old brother was also adopted, but from within the US. Jaden had dark curly hair and light brown skin. In her family, only Grace was Chinese. She had Asian friends in school, a few born in other countries, and most born in America. But now she was someplace where almost everyone looked like her. It would be fun to be in the majority for once!

She was too tired the night before to take in much of what she saw. Today, they would stop by an orphanage to drop off some gifts from the US. Then Dad, Jaden, and Grace would spend three days hiking along the Great Wall of China. After that they would spend time in Beijing. Grace didn't remember any of her life in China. Would she feel at home now?

They went down the elevator to the hotel lobby. The hotel was a tall building with lots of shiny, mirrored glass. It did not look Chinese, except for the signs in both Chinese and English. The nearby buildings also looked like those in any other city. Was China just like every other place?

They got into a taxi. The streets were packed with people walking or driving or on their bicycles. The whole city was practically one big traffic jam.

Nearly all of the people they passed were Chinese. Grace studied them curiously. What if

her birth parents were there? Grace was left at an orphanage when she was only a few days old. She could not remember any of her life before coming to America. She would see her birth country, but her parents warned her that she wouldn't learn anything about her Chinese family.

Still, she liked the idea that she might pass by them somewhere. She imagined seeing her mother or father and just knowing who they were.

They got out at the orphanage. Her father put his arm around Grace and kissed the top of her head. Well, she knew who her real parents were! They took care of her every day. But she was curious about her birth parents, too. Who were they? Did they look like her? Why had they given her up for adoption?

A friendly Chinese woman led them into a sitting room.

"Welcome! Thank you for your visit." She waved them to seats. "I apologize, but I cannot show you the rest of the orphanage. It is against the rules."

"We understand," Dad said. "We wanted to leave this box of gifts donated by some of our friends in the United States."

While Dad and the woman talked, Jaden whispered, "Maybe we can leave you here and no one will notice." Grace stuck her tongue out at him.

"How are things here?" Dad asked.

Ms. Chun said, "We have some lovely volunteers from America working here for the summer. We need a lot of help. Ten years ago, most of our children were healthy baby girls." She smiled at Grace. "China is very crowded, with over a billion people, so the government only allows most families to have one child. Boys were most valued."

"Boys are better," Jaden said. He grinned at Grace and she made a face.

"Jaden, don't tease your sister," Dad said. "You know that boys and girls are both equally the best."

Ms. Chun went on.

"The tradition was that women go live with their husband's family when they marry. People with no sons had no one to take care of the parents in their old age. People who had a girl first sometimes gave her up, so they could try again for a son."

Grace leaned close to her father and whispered, "I'll take care of you, Daddy."

"Thanks, but we don't have to worry about that

for a long time," he whispered back.

"In the past few years, things have changed," Ms. Chun said. "People see the value of girls and keep their girl babies. Also, rich Chinese couples will adopt the healthy baby girls. This way they can have more than one child legally. This is good, but it means now most of the children here have serious health problems. Poor families cannot afford to take care of these children, so they give them up. It would be better if the government helped the poor people take care of their children at home. So far, that is not the case."

Dad pulled a photo out of his pocket and passed it to Ms. Chun. "I know the little girl we are adopting, Joy, is going to need at least one surgery, maybe more."

"Why can't we get a normal kid?" Jaden asked.

"There's no such thing," Dad said, ruffling his hair. "You are all exceptional."

Ms. Chun handed the photo back. She told Grace, "I hope you will enjoy having a little sister. You will be her jie jie. That means big sister. She will be your mei mei. That means little sister. We give the children all the care and love we have, but a child deserves a forever family. That is why we are so grateful for people like you!" She stood up. "The children will enjoy these gifts."

They said their goodbyes and went out. "Let's walk and look for someplace to have lunch," Dad said. The three of them went down the street hand-in-hand.

"Dad," Grace whispered, "do you think my parents gave me up because they didn't want a girl?"

"I don't know, sweetheart. Maybe they were too poor or one of them was sick." He put his arm around her. "I think they wanted you to have a better life than they could give you. Whatever the reason, we are very glad you came to us." Grace felt warm inside.

They passed through crowds of people. Lots of them smiled at Grace. Now that she was seeing everyone close up, most of them didn't look that much like her. She had light brown eyes and just a touch of curl to her black hair. There was a lot of variety here. Still, Dad was the one who stood out in this crowd. Jaden, too, but he was short so people didn't notice him as much.

A few minutes later, they found a restaurant to try. Dad looked at the menu, which listed things in English as well as Chinese. "Let's see. Do you want deep-fried sparrow? Spicy sliced mule?"

Grace made a face.

"How about some fish?" Dad said.

"Yes please!"

The fish came whole, with the head and tail still attached. Dad pulled it apart and put a little on Grace's and Jaden's plates. Grace asked him to turn the fish away so it wasn't staring at her. They also had some roast duck, noodles, and steamed pork buns. It was good, but it wasn't quite like the Chinese food Grace had back home. Was that food Americanized Chinese, like she was?

"Dad, can I see the picture of Joy?" He handed

it over and she studied the two-year-old girl in a pink jumpsuit and thick glasses. This little girl was Chinese. Grace was Chinese-American. Her parents bought her a lot of books about China. She had read some Chinese folktales and historical fiction set in China. Her favorites novels were modern stories about Chinese-American girls like herself. She thought she knew all about China, but now that she was there, she realized she didn't. Grace felt much more American than Chinese, especially here in China.

Joy would probably only know Chinese words. Grace had learned a few words in Chinese, but not many. How was Grace supposed to be a big sister when they did not even speak the same language?

Chapter Two

Alone in a Crowd

Grace and Jaden each had a small backpack, while Dad had a larger one. They met up with their hired guide in the hotel lobby. The guide said his name was Danny. He had another Chinese name, but he said Danny was easier for Americans.

A taxi took them beyond the city. For the next three days, they would hike along the Great Wall of China. Dad was going to write an article about the experience. Jaden would probably spend the time causing as much trouble as he could. And Grace would get to see more of the country where she'd been born. Maybe by the end, she would know how to be a big sister to Joy.

They crossed a plaza toward a square stone structure several stories high. On top of the square stone part was a red tower with balconies and fancy eaves sticking out. The building had a tunnel running right through the middle, all the way to the other side.

Several people were taking photos in front of the stone building. Dad took pictures of Grace and Jaden. Then the guide, Danny, took a picture of all three of them.

Dad and Danny stopped at the ticket counter. Jaden ran ahead through the tunnel. Dad called out, "Jaden, not too far!" He sighed. "Grace..." She nodded and ran after Jaden. Her brother had a way of not hearing instructions.

The other side of the tunnel was crowded with people. A group of Chinese teenagers in white track suits with red and blue stripes pushed past her. Where was Jaden? Grace squirmed among the crowd, trying to find him. No luck. She headed back for the tunnel opening. But where were her father and the guide? She didn't recognize anyone in the huge crowd.

A girl about Grace's age smiled and said something. Grace did not understand a word. Grace gave her a little smile and shook her head. All around her, voices rose and fell, making no sense. The few words of Chinese she knew seemed useless. Grace blinked back tears.

She needed to ask for help. A few feet away, a man was selling maps of the wall. Maybe he spoke some English. Grace approached him. "Excuse me, do you speak English?"

He stared at her for a moment. "American?" When she nodded, he thrust a map at her. "Map. You want?"

"I don't need a map. My dad and guide –"

He interrupted. "Cards? Postcard is five yuan." He held out a bunch of postcards.

Grace backed up. "No. I need –" But the man kept chattering. Maybe he didn't understand, since he only seemed to know a few words of English. Grace turned and ran away.

Other people were selling bottled water and soft drinks. Different languages filled the air. Someone bumped against Grace and said something in Chinese. Did they think she was a local? She didn't feel at home here; she felt lost and alone.

Grace worked her way over to the edge of the plaza and leaned against the wall. She was too short to see over people's heads, but at least she wasn't in the middle of a crowd. But would her father ever find her there? With so many people, he might be twenty feet away and they would not see each other.

Back home, she might look for a police officer. Here, she didn't know what would happen if she found one. Would he understand her? Would she get in trouble for being alone? What did the police look like here, anyway?

If she found something to stand on, maybe she could see over the crowd. She spotted a steep flight of stone steps. People streamed up and down them, but it was not quite as crowded as at the bottom. Grace ran for the steps and went partway up. She turned and scanned the crowd below. It should be easy to spot her father, because he was taller than most of the Chinese.

She thought she saw her father's brown hair, but when the man turned, it was someone else. Actually, there were a lot of tall men who were not Chinese. They must be tourists from other countries.

Her father would be wearing a blue jacket and a large backpack. Grace kept looking.

There he was! He was turning and looking in

all directions, but he didn't seem to see Grace. She needed to attract his attention.

She looked down at her own red jacket. She slipped off her small backpack and took off the jacket. Then she waved the jacket back and forth above her head.

Finally Dad turned and waved to her.

Grace lowered her arm and leaned against the wall. She let out a big sigh. That had been scary, and they hadn't even started their hike! She wasn't sure she liked this place. She wanted to be back home, where she knew her way around and people understood her.

Dad and the guide joined her. Grace gave her father a hug and said, "I'm sorry, I lost Jaden."

He kissed the top of her head. "He's right behind you."

Grace turned to see Jaden bouncing down the steps toward them. "Come on, what are you waiting for?" he said.

Grace chuckled. She was too relieved to be angry. She should have known Jaden would start without them.

They hiked up the steep steps. Grace's legs

ached a little by the end. They reached a flat area big enough for five or six people to stand side by side. It stretched into the distance, as far as the eye could see. They were on top of the Great Wall of China! On either side of the flat top, smaller walls rose to head height to keep people from falling off. It was a wall with walls.

Grace could hardly see anything with all the tourists. Dad led them to the edge of the wall where there was a rectangular gap in the stone. They looked out at the wall running along the tops of forested hills. In the distance a tower rose up from the wall. Its gray stones and arched openings looked like a medieval castle.

Dad pointed to where the wall disappeared in the distance. "That's where we're heading. Come on, let's get away from these crowds."

"Too many people," Danny said. "You feel like dumplings in a pot! But most people do not go more than a mile along the wall. Soon we will be alone."

They wormed their way past people blocking the aisle to take pictures. Grace heard many different languages. Some people were wearing

shorts or skirts and sandals, clearly not planning a big hike. Grace glanced down at her hiking boots. Good thing they had broken in the boots with lots of practice hikes at home, so the boots wouldn't pinch or rub.

Soon the heavy crowds dwindled. Only a few other people had ventured that far, so their group could walk side-by-side most of the time. Jaden ran ahead, but they could see him. Grace smiled up at her father and took his hand. Maybe this place wasn't so bad after all.

Chapter Three

The Dragon's Back

As they walked, Danny told them about the wall.

"Most tourists only see a mile or two of the wall. You will see more, but it will still be only a tiny part of the whole wall."

They came to a place where the wall curved around, going up a hill ahead. They stopped to look through the openings in the side wall. "We call it the Great Wall but it is really many walls," Danny said. He pointed into the distance. "In some places, the wall stops at a mountain or cliff. There the land becomes a natural barrier. In other places, two or three walls run side by side. If the enemy gets past one wall, he faces another."

"Can't we walk the whole thing?" Jaden asked.

Danny and their father both laughed. "The wall is 5,500 miles long," Dad said. "That's like walking from Seattle to New York City and back again!"

Jaden's eyes widened. Grace tried to imagine walking all the way across America. It would take months!

"Actually, the wall is even longer," Danny said. "Many books still say 5,500 miles. That is from history records. But they made a survey a few years ago. If you count all the walls, from all the times in history, there are more than 13,000 miles of wall."

Their father frowned. "That doesn't even seem possible. China is about the same size as America. The US is only about 3,000 miles across."

"But you must remember, the wall does not go in a straight line." Danny wove his hand through the air like a snake. "It twists and turns, and it goes up and down hills."

"Oh, that makes sense." Dad nodded. "It covers a lot more ground than if you drew a line on a map."

Grace wasn't sure she understood all that. But one thing was clear: The Great Wall of China was very, very long! She was glad they were only hiking for a few days.

Jaden boosted himself up on a low spot on the wall. Dad grabbed the back of his jacket to hold him.

Danny said, "There are also branches off the main wall, plus the places where several walls run parallel. Maybe someday we will say the wall is even longer. They found a new part a few years ago. Another 180 miles! It was mostly collapsed, and it was in a remote area, so they did not know it was there before. More of the wall could still be hidden."

Jaden twisted around and bounced down to the ground. "Let's go find it!"

Danny and Dad laughed again. "I don't think we have time on this trip," Dad said. "But maybe you can come back someday and find it."

Danny stepped back.

"We say the wall is like a mighty stone dragon!" He gestured in one direction. "The dragon's head sits at the edge of the Yellow Sea." He gestured in the other direction. "Its tail extends west. Legend says that a helpful dragon showed where to build the wall."

They began walking again. Dad jotted notes in a little notebook while Danny talked. "Parts of the wall were built more than 2,000 years ago. Even before that, there were walls for defense. But they were small and not connected. The first Emperor of China, Qin Shi Huang, started the big wall-building project. Other dynasties added to the wall."

"What are dynasties?" Grace asked.

Dad answered. "A dynasty is a family that rules for a long time. Maybe one man conquers the land. When he dies, his son takes over as ruler. Then his grandson, then his great-grandson. Or sometimes a daughter."

Danny nodded. "When a new family takes over, it is a new dynasty," he said. "In China, some families ruled for hundreds of years. But most of the wall you can see today was built during the Ming Dynasty. That was about 500 years ago."

Grace wandered ahead as the men kept talking. She was walking on something built 500 years ago! It was hard to imagine.

Jaden was getting ahead of them. Grace hurried to catch up. She knew her father got distracted when he was working on an article. And Jaden could get in trouble the moment he was left alone. Grace was only two years older, and she was the responsible one. Mom said Grace was ten going on 30. Jaden was eight but often acted younger.

Jaden stopped at one of the openings in the wall. He boosted himself up and stuck his head and shoulders out the opening. Grace grabbed the back of his jacket, like her father had done.

"What are you doing?" she asked.

"I want to get down on the ground, but the wall is too high here."

"Jaden! You can't leave the wall."

"You're not the boss of me!"

Grace looked back down the wall. Her father and Danny were within shouting distance. She looked over Jaden's shoulder. The wall sloped down at a slight angle to the ground. But it was far too steep for even Jaden to think he could slide down it. Trees grew nearby, but not within reach. For the moment, her brother's plans were foiled, so she didn't need to yell for Dad. But it might be a good idea to distract Jaden before he found some other kind of trouble.

"I'll race you back to Dad." Grace let go of Jaden and started running. She smiled as she heard her brother's footsteps pounding after her. He could never resist a challenge. She slowed just enough to let Jaden reach Dad at the same time.

Dad staggered backward as they barreled into him. "Whoa! What's all the commotion?"

"Just a race," Grace said.

Dad smiled. "We have a lot of hiking to do, so don't wear yourselves out," he said.

"Race you back!" Jaden yelled as he took off.

Grace groaned and ran after him. At least he'd forgotten about trying to get to the ground, for the moment.

The day got hotter. They stopped for a picnic lunch in a watchtower. Grace and Jaden ran around the columns and looked through the arched openings. Green mountains rolled in the distance. "This is very well preserved for being so old," Dad said. "Or has it been repaired?"

"It was rebuilt," Danny said. "Near the cities, they make the wall nice for the tourists. As we go farther, you will see more ruins."

"Makes sense. Hey, is it true that the Great Wall is the only man-made structure you can see from space?"

"No, that is not true," Danny said. "The wall is only 12 feet wide in most places. Most highways are wider."

"Another myth busted." Dad sighed and eased his backpack to the ground. He sat on a stone windowsill and reached for his boot. "I think I'm getting a blister. I'd better tape it."

Jaden ran up a steep flight of stairs to the upper level. "Jaden, hold on a minute," Dad said, his boot in one hand.

"I'll watch him," Grace said. She started to follow, but glanced back when her dad said something. "What?"

"I said be careful."

"Okay." Grace trotted up the stairs. The top of the tower was about 20 feet across in each direction. Around the edge the narrow stone wall rose up, a parapet to keep people from falling off. A small stone building stood in the center of the tower top. Grace could not immediately see Jaden.

He must be either in the little building or on the other side, she thought.

She went around the building. No Jaden outside the building. She found the doorway and peeked in. No Jaden inside either. Surely he could not have tried to get over the wall! It was a long drop down, and no trees grew close enough to reach. He must have slipped past her and back down the stairway.

Then she heard a noise from above. A bird or animal on the roof of the little building? Grace backed up so she could see. The building had a peaked roof. One side sloped down toward her. At first she didn't see anything.

Then Jaden's head popped up at the top of the roof. He had somehow climbed onto the top of the building!

Chapter Four

Buried Ghosts

Grace raced around to the other side of the building. Jaden was standing on the slope of the roof. He was holding onto the ridge where the two sides of the peaked roof met. "Jaden, what are you doing?" Looking up at him above her head, the building no longer seemed so small. If Jaden slid off the roof, he would have a bad fall.

Jaden said, "I can see a million miles!"

"Well, come back down! You could fall." Where was Dad? Grace wanted to look for him, but she could not take her eyes off Jaden.

Jaden turned and looked down at Grace. He wobbled for a moment, let out a strange sound, and collapsed against the roof. He held onto the ridge as if his life depended on it. Maybe it did.

Grace tried to speak calmly. "Come down."

"I can't!"

Grace's heart was pounding hard. She felt a little dizzy just looking up at Jaden. But she had to stay calm and help. "How did you get up there?"

Jaden didn't answer. His eyes were wide and scared. That scared Grace, too, because Jaden was hardly ever scared of anything.

Men's voices came from the other side of the small building. Grace's heart leapt. Dad would know what to do! But she couldn't leave Jaden alone for even a second. If he fell, she would have to break his fall to save him, even if it squashed her flat. She called out, "Dad, come here quick!"

Her father hurried around the corner of the building. "What's wrong?" He looked where Grace was pointing. "Jaden!"

Grace moved aside as her father got underneath Jaden. Dad lifted his arms up and touched the edge of the roof. "Jaden, work your way down to me slowly."

"I can't," Jaden whimpered.

"Of course you can," Dad said. "Just slide down the roof, slowly, and I'll catch you."

Danny came to stand beside Dad. Grace crossed her fingers on both hands as she watched them. Her brother was a pain, but she did not want him hurt.

Finally Jaden started sliding down the roof, a few inches at a time. Dad could reach his foot. Then Jaden was at the edge of the roof and Dad grabbed his waist. A moment later Dad had Jaden in a big hug. Dad comforted him for a moment, and then he put Jaden down and gave him a serious scolding.

Grace turned away and looked out over the landscape. The green hills were soothing, but when she looked down to the ground below, she had to take a step back. Now it seemed like they were up too high.

Dad put a hand on her shoulder. "Come on, let's go down to have our lunch."

Jaden was quiet as they ate the food they packed. For once, he stayed close to his family. Danny told them about the watchtowers while they ate bread, sausage, bananas, and potato chips.

"The Emperors built this wall to keep out invaders. There were thousands of watchtowers. Each would have a dozen soldiers. They had rooms for sleeping and a room for cooking."

Grace looked around at the stone walls. This was a pretty comfortable place to have lunch, but she didn't think she would want to live there.

"It must have gotten cold in the winter," Dad said.

Danny nodded. "Yes, although they would have had wooden shutters and doors to keep out the wind."

"A dozen soldiers isn't very many to defend the wall," Dad said. Jaden got up and went to one of the arched windows. He pretended to draw back a bow and let an arrow fly.

"They had fortresses to guard important towns," Danny said. "Forts also defended river crossings and passages through the mountains."

Jaden turned from the window. "What did the

soldiers do here if they didn't fight?"

"They watched from the towers and they sent messages if they saw the enemy coming." Danny waved toward the stairway to the top of the tower. "They used straw and dung to make fires up there."

"Dung?" Jaden asked. "You mean, poop?"

Danny nodded and Jaden burst into laughter. Danny smiled.

"They used dung from the sheep and cattle they raised for food. But the best dung was supposed to be wolf dung. The smoke was called langyan, which means wolves' smoke."

Dad scribbled in his notebook as Danny went on. "During the day, they could use smoke to send signals. At night, the fire was the signal. Other watchtowers could see the smoke or fire. They also used cannons to make noises. The number of smoke signals and cannon booms told how many people were attacking."

Danny got up and pointed out the stone window. Grace and Jaden stood beside him, looking out at the wall. It was a gray stone stripe going up and down through the green hills to another watchtower in the distance.

"Look how far you can see," Danny said. "The smoke signals were faster than horsemen. One time they did a test. They tried horses, Jeeps, and smoke. In this rough country, the smoke signals were fastest. The Jeeps could not even get through, because their wheels got bogged down in the mud."

Danny sat down again. "The wall was also a road. Soldiers could run along the wall to wherever they were needed. It was safer and faster than running across the land. So if one tower signaled for help, other soldiers would come."

Grace looked out the window. She imagined soldiers running along the wall. Were they afraid? Did they get bored if no one invaded? She turned back to Danny. "Were there any girl soldiers?"

"Yes, of course. Several women led armies into battle. Many royal women were good archers. Some were also excellent at martial arts fighting."

"You mean like karate or kung fu?" Grace asked.

"No way!" Jaden said. "Not girls."

Danny tapped him on the nose.

"Yes! Although the term kung fu means something different in China. Basically, it means time spent at hard training or skillful work.

Because martial arts requires much hard training, the term got attached to it. Here we call it wu shu, which means the art of war. Wu shu is the national sport of China, but it is no longer so much about war."

"It's cool that a lot of women did it," Grace turned to Jaden. "And for your information, Samantha in my class at school takes karate and she's the best in her age group!"

He gave her a sheepish grin, and she knew he'd been teasing again.

"There was even an army of women led by a princess," Danny said. "The local ruler saw Lin Siniang practicing martial arts and fell in love with her. He made her a princess and she taught the women of the royal court martial arts. When the king was captured, she led the women in an attempt to rescue him. Then there was Xun Guan, the daughter of a governor. Rebels surrounded the city and the governor needed help. Xun Guan led a small team at night as they rode out of the city and broke through enemy lines. She was only 13 years old."

"Did she succeed?" Grace asked breathlessly.

"Yes, and she was hailed as a hero," Danny said. "But not all stories are so happy. Mu Guiying was an expert in martial arts. When her husband was killed, Mu Guiying led all the widows of her clan into war. They fought bravely but the enemy killed all the women. They were buried where they died, near a cliff. It is said that the Dowager She, the female head of the family, wept at the tomb. The mountain spirit wept tears of sympathy. These became boulders that rolled down the cliff. The area is now called Rolling Tears Cliff."

He began packing away the garbage from their lunches. "There are many other stories of brave Chinese women fighting. You may know the movie Mulan. It is based on a true story about a girl who disguised herself as a boy and went into battle."

"And she's just the one we know about," Dad said. "There may have been other girls who disguised themselves and were never found out." He stood. "Shall we get going?"

They walked out onto the top of the wall again. It was hard to imagine soldiers and invaders here. It was quiet and peaceful. The trees rustled, and a few birds sang. They had gotten away from the other tourists. They were almost alone under the blue sky, with green hills all around.

Dad paused to take a photo. "The wall is so picturesque, I want to capture every part of it in pictures," he said. "It's no wonder the wall is the symbol of China."

Danny nodded. "It is a source of pride, but the wall was built at a great cost. Many people died building it," he said.

Jaden, who had been running ahead, turned back and walked next to Danny. "How did they die?" he asked.

"It was difficult work. Over three million people labored on the wall. Soldiers did a lot of the work, but the worst jobs they saved for prisoners. Many people were worked to death. It is said they were tossed into the middle of the wall and buried in the rubble. Some say a million people died making it."

Jaden's eyes were big. "You mean we're walking on top of dead bodies?"

Danny shrugged. "Maybe. That is the story. They have not found all these bones in the wall. Still, the wall is called the longest cemetery on earth."

Jaden grabbed Grace's arm. "We're going to camp

on the wall! Above dead men. I bet there will be ghosts at night." He made a spooky howling sound.

"Stop it," Grace said. She didn't believe in ghosts. But she didn't want to think about sleeping above dead people, either.

They met a few tourists, but these were different from the people back at the beginning. Everyone was a hiker, like Grace's family, and had big backpacks. Most of them were kind of dirty from sleeping outside. Some of the men had scruffy beards, like they hadn't shaved in days. Dad greeted everyone. If they spoke English, he chatted for a while. Some were Americans. Other tourists came from Europe. Some were Chinese getting away from the city.

They hiked throughout the afternoon. Sometimes they passed farm fields or cottages. Jaden mostly walked with Danny. They were probably talking about ghosts and fighting and dung. Grace kept her distance and took pictures with the camera she got for her birthday. Dad took pictures as well. They didn't hike too fast, but Grace's feet and legs started to hurt. Her backpack seemed heavier than when they started. It was a lot of walking for one day.

Later in the afternoon, clouds blew in. They got

thicker and grayer, and the wind whipped Grace's hair into her face. At first the breeze was a nice break from the heat, but then Grace started to shiver. She paused to put on her jacket.

A while later, Danny and Jaden waited for Dad and Grace to catch up. Danny looked worried. "I think it will rain soon. We need to hurry so we can get to the next village," he said.

"Really?" Dad said. "The forecast was only a 30 percent chance of rain. I was hoping we could camp in a watchtower tonight."

Danny shook his head.

"It is not safe during a storm. There can be much lightning. The wall is the highest thing around, so it gets hit by lightning very often."

Dad looked at Grace and Jaden. "Okay, I guess we want to get off the wall. How far to the village?"

"Maybe half an hour," Danny said. "Maybe an hour. We have been going slowly."

Dad looked at the sky. "How long before it starts to rain?"

"Very soon, I think," Danny said. "Less than one hour."

Dad nodded. "We'd better hurry."

Chapter Five

Mirrors in the Sky

Grace held onto her backpack straps to keep the pack from bouncing. She was tired and her legs felt heavy. They'd already walked for hours. Danny hurried ahead of the group. Jaden ran beside him for a few minutes but then dropped back again. Dad was a few feet ahead of her; he kept turning and waving for Grace to hurry. Easy for him to say, he had long legs!

At least walking quickly helped keep her warm. The wind bit at her face and ears. Her nose was running and she couldn't even stop to blow it. She glanced through a gap in the wall. The trees on the hill below were shaking in the wind.

They were now alone on the wall. The other hikers had all probably found shelter already. Thunder rumbled in the distance. Grace didn't see any lightning, but it had to be there. They learned in school that if you heard thunder, lightning was making the sound. Lightning was electricity, and it usually hit tall things. Often that was a tree, building, or mountain.

Right now, it was them, on the wall.

Rain sprinkled her face, making it harder to see. For a moment she lost sight of the others. Grace started to run. She glimpsed a dark figure ahead. As she got closer she recognized her father. He scooped her up in his arms and carried her for a minute. When they reached Jaden, Dad put her down and took their hands. They ran together side-by-side.

The rain grew heavier. A flash of lightning lit the sky. A few seconds later, thunder boomed.

Danny waved to them from up ahead. Then he disappeared – one second there, the next gone. Had the wall collapsed from all the rain?

They reached the spot where Danny had disappeared. Stairs went down off the wall.

"Careful," Dad said as they scrambled down. "The stone could be slippery."

It was slippery, even in hiking boots that were

made to grip. Grace held onto the wall on one side and stepped carefully.

Boom! The lightning flashed and crackled. Dad grabbed Grace with one arm and Jaden with the other and pulled them down so they huddled together at the base of the steps. For a few seconds, the thunder echoed in Grace's ears and she saw spots. The air had a strange smell, and she felt tingly, but maybe that was from being scared.

"That was too close," Dad said. "Let's go!"

Danny pushed his wet hair out of his eyes and said, "We will go to a farmer near here. He built rooms for tourists to stay in. You will find it very comfortable."

"Better than this, anyway!" Dad said.

Thunder rumbled like an army on the march. Flashes of lightning lit the distant clouds, turning them purple. The ground was soft and muddy, sucking at their feet. Grass and bushes sprinkled more water onto their clothes. Good thing they had packed their extra clothes inside plastic bags, in their backpacks!

Everyone was soaked by the time they reached the farm. Danny and the farmer talked in Chinese.

Then the man showed them to a long building. The rooms had hard beds and bare floors, but they were dry. Everyone changed into dry clothes. They met up outside and sat at tables under an awning. A garden surrounded the picnic area. Grace saw cucumbers and green beans growing nearby. Many of the other vegetables she did not recognize. Simply seeing food made Grace realize how hungry she was. Her stomach grumbled.

A few minutes later, their host brought out plates heaped with food. Danny helped identify what they were eating. "This is beans and pork. Here is potatoes and peppers. They grow the food right here in the garden," he said.

Grace's family went out for Chinese food at least once a month. Sometimes Dad cooked a dish he called Chinese stir fry. This food was different, though. Little dumplings were stuffed with scrambled eggs. One pot held a broth with vegetables and thin slices of mutton. Mutton was from sheep. Grace couldn't remember ever eating sheep before. The dish was so spicy she had to blow her nose three times while she ate. But it made her feel nice and warm inside.

A few things looked so strange that she didn't even want to try them. She had plenty to eat anyway. Jaden tried everything, the weirder the better. She knew he was going to go home and brag to his friend about the strange things he'd tasted. For dessert they had a sweet, chewy pastry. Grace had started out very hungry. By the end of dinner, she was stuffed!

"Xie xie," Grace said. She'd learned how to say thank you in Chinese, pronounced sort of like "shay shay," from a video. It was hard, because the first word started high and then dropped lower. The second word was a single tone.

Jaden turned to their host and said "Xie xie," and then something Grace didn't understand. The farmer bowed and smiled. He said something back in Chinese.

"What was that?" Grace asked.

"I told him the food was good," Jaden said proudly. "Danny taught me." He showed off a few more words of Chinese. So they hadn't only been talking about dead bodies and ghosts!

"He is very good," Danny said. "It is hard for Westerners to learn Chinese."

"I'll say," Dad said. "We tried to learn some before our first visit here, when we came for Grace. The language is so different, and how you say words makes a difference. I couldn't get that part."

Danny nodded. "The meaning changes if you say a word with a rising or falling sound. But Jaden does this very well."

Dad looked impressed. "Maybe you have a gift for languages," he said to Jaden.

"It's no big deal." Jaden shrugged, but his smile showed he was pleased.

It didn't seem fair. Grace was born in China! She should be the one who found Chinese easy.

How could Jaden be more at home here than she was? But then again, she hadn't actually tried to learn any of the language except a few basic words, such as hello, please and thank you.

"Teach me how to say something else," Jaden said.

Danny turned to him. "If you are angry at someone, you can say 'tian da lei pi.' This translates to 'sky beat thunder strike.' You are hoping the person will be struck by thunder."

Jaden turned to Grace with a glint in his eye.

"Don't you dare!" she said. "Not with the storm."

Jaden looked at Dad, seeming to judge how much trouble he would get into. He sighed. "The storm is stopping anyway," he said.

Thunder rumbled again, but the lightning was far off now and not so scary. Danny said, "The Chinese have a legend about thunder and lightning."

Dad got out his notebook and pencil.

"Long ago, there was no lightning during a storm, only thunder," Danny said. "The thunder was from the God of Thunder, when he killed evil people. But one night, he made a mistake. He killed a good woman. The Jade Emperor brought the woman back to life. He made her the Goddess of Lightning. She had two lightning mirrors. These showed whether someone was good or evil. She would use these mirrors to judge people. Only then could the God of Thunder punish the evil ones. This is why we see a flash of lightning before hearing thunder."

"But thunder doesn't kill people," Jaden said. "It's the lightning that's dangerous."

Danny shrugged. "We know that now," he said.

"It's still a good story," Grace said. She wanted Danny to like her as much as he liked Jaden. But it was an interesting story too. Maybe she would keep her own journal of Chinese legends. She could write about women warriors and goddesses!

"You just like that story because it's about a girl," Jaden said.

Danny was watching, so Grace did not stick her tongue out at her brother. Sometimes she wished she had a sister.

She remembered with a shock that she would have a sister! Grace would be jie jie, big sister to her mei mei, Joy. She would have a sister from

China. *Xie xie*, she thought, *thank you.*

Grace turned to look out over the land. It had gotten dark while they talked, but the rain had stopped. She could barely hear thunder far away. The storm had moved on.

Something swooped over Grace's head. She gasped as it flew into the night. "What was that?"

"A bat!" Jaden said. He curved two fingers up by his mouth like long fangs. "A vampire bat, and it's going to eat you!"

Grace sniffed. "Bats are good. They eat insects and pollinate flowers so they grow. A lot of fruit trees depend on bats." She'd learned that in school. "And there are no real vampires."

Jaden wasn't listening. He'd hopped up to run around the table holding his arms out like wings.

Their host paused from cleaning up the dishes. "Swallow," he said.

Grace looked at him. Why did she need to swallow? She'd finished eating.

The man nodded and pointed to the edge of the roof. "Swallow brings good luck. Good for house."

Danny said, "The swallow is a symbol of spring, because the birds return every spring. If a swallow nests in a Chinese house, we do not disturb them. It is considered good luck."

Oh, the bird swallow, not the thing you did in your throat, she thought. In the shadows of the lantern, Grace could just make out the nest. It looked like a lump of clay stuck to the house close to the eaves. It would be cool to have a swallow living at your house.

"The Chinese have a lot of symbolism about animals, right?" Dad said.

Danny nodded. "The dragon has many meanings. One is good fortune, and it is also the symbol for the Emperor. The bat is also good luck. Deer mean wealth and long life. A cricket shows the fighting spirit."

"A cricket!" Jaden laughed. "How can a little bug be a mean fighter?"

"The cricket is a strong fighter," Danny said. "People keep crickets in special cages. They watch two crickets fight. It is a popular sport, like your football! The Chinese people have done this for many centuries."

"Cool!" Jaden said. "Can I get a cricket? No, two, so they can fight."

"I don't think you'll be able to take an animal back to the US," Dad said.

Grace frowned. "Do the crickets kill each other?" she asked.

Danny shook his head. "The fight is done when one cricket overcomes the other. They do not usually kill each other. Crickets are also kept for their singing. Over a thousand years ago, the ladies in the palace would catch crickets. They would put the crickets in small golden cages by their pillow. At night, they could hear the cricket's song."

Maybe having a cricket would be nice after all. But Jaden would probably try to teach it to fight. Grace yawned. Suddenly she wanted to fall asleep. It had been a long day. And they had another long day ahead.

Chapter Six

What's in the Wall?

They had a breakfast of steamed buns. Grace said thank you in Chinese to the farmer. He bowed and said something back she did not understand. But she smiled and bowed as well.

Jaden started running around the garden while Dad loaded up his pack. He had to wait for water to boil so he could refill the water bottles, otherwise the water would not be safe for them to drink. Boiling it killed the bacteria that might make them sick. Danny and the farmer were packing food for lunch.

Dad glanced up as Jaden raced past, nearly knocking into their host. "If you two want to run ahead, okay. But wait for us on the wall. See that tower?" He pointed across the fields. Trees, bushes, and a low-lying fog partly hid the gray wall, but a tower rose up above everything. "We'll meet there."

Jaden took off and Grace ran after him. The fields were still soft from the night rain, and mud stuck to her shoes. The air was moist with humidity. Ahead of them, wisps of fog shrouded the wall.

Jaden reached the forested strip along the wall ahead of her. "Wait up!" Grace called. Jaden stopped and looked back. Maybe he was learning to be more cautious in a strange place.

Grace reached Jaden and they went in among the trees. The light was dimmer with the branches overhead. Bushes snagged at their clothes. Grace glanced back. She could no longer see the farmer's house, or even the field. But ahead of them, glimpses of gray stone showed through gaps in the trees. The wall would be easy to find.

Grace paused to free her sleeve from a bush that had grabbed it.

"I don't remember it being like this last night," she said. Didn't they come down from the wall on a path? She wasn't sure. She had been tired and nervous, and the rain had made it hard to see.

They came to the wall. Gray stone stretched out left and right. The wall rose up 20 feet high, far above their heads. They could not see a path or stairs anywhere.

"Oops," Grace said. "I guess we came to the wrong place." She looked down the wall to the left. She looked down the wall to the right. With the trees and bushes growing close to the wall, she couldn't see very far. Which way were the stairs?

"I can climb up!" Jaden said. He put his hands on the wall. It sloped slightly away from them, but the slope was very steep and the stones in the wall fit close together.

"No!" Grace said. "You'll slide right back down." She turned to look away from the wall. If they went back to the farm field, they could wait for Dad and Danny there. But what if they got lost among the trees? They could go in circles for days!

Grace shuddered. She did not want to be lost. She especially did not want to be lost in a strange place, with only her brother for company. Still, maybe being with him was better than being alone.

They could shout and wait for Dad to find them. It might take a long time. He and Danny probably used the correct path, and they might be too far away to hear Grace and Jaden yell.

They could try to go back to the farm. They had been able to see the wall from among the trees. So if they kept walking away from the wall, eventually they would get back to the fields. But would she recognize the right farmer's house? Besides, Dad and Danny might be at the wall by that time.

They were supposed to meet at the stairs. Dad would worry if they weren't there. Grace took a deep breath. "We have to find the stairs," she said.

She backed up to try to see the wall better. The light was brighter to her left. She grabbed Jaden's hand and moved over there into a small clearing. With fewer trees, she could see more of the wall. To the right, a watchtower rose up.

"There's the tower! I'll bet there are stairs up to the tower, because the soldiers would need to get up and down. Come on."

They squirmed between the bushes and the wall. In a few minutes, the forest opened up at stone stairs leading to the tower. Dad and Danny were coming up the path from the field. Dad waved.

"What are you doing?" he asked.

"Oh, just exploring." Grace grinned. She and Jaden led the way up the stairs.

It was nice being back on top of the wall after being in the bushes. The path was wide and open. The ground steamed as the sun warmed the air and the fog burned off. Then they could see for miles on either side of the wall. The wall went up hills and down valleys, a gray snake among the green hills.

Jaden ran ahead. Grace did not want to chase after him all day! She was happy to walk beside Dad.

Dad called out, "Hey, Jaden, hold up! I heard something you'll find interesting. Do you know what they used to make the mortar for the wall?"

Jaden turned and came back. "What's mortar?"

"It's the glue that holds the stones together." Dad put his arm around Jaden's shoulder. "I heard that it's made from crushed human bones!"

Jaden's eyes got big. "No way!"

Yuck, Grace thought.

Danny chuckled. "That is a good story, but I am afraid it is not true." When Jaden looked disappointed, the guide said, "But the truth is also very interesting. The mortar is made from rice flour."

Jaden made a face. "It's made from flowers?"

Grace shook her head. It figured he would find

that weirder than mortar made from bones. "Flour, like you make bread with. Right?"

"That's right," Danny said. "During the Ming Dynasty, they made very good bricks. They are as strong as what we make today. They needed a strong mortar to hold the bricks together. The mortar is made from powdered sticky rice."

Grace thought about that. It wasn't so different from making paper mâché from flour and water. They had made a paper mâché volcano in science. They soaked strips of newspaper in the flour and water paste. Once it dried, it was very hard.

Jaden poked at the thin seam between two bricks.

"Careful, you don't want to damage anything," Dad said.

Jaden sighed. "It would be cooler if it was made from bones."

"You like stories of death?" Danny said. "One legend says that a farmer died on the wall. His wife was so sad that she went to the wall and cried. The wall collapsed under the weight of her grief. Then she found his bones and buried him."

Jaden considered for a minute. "Girl stuff," he decided. "But I'd like to see the wall collapse." He threw out his arms. "Boom! Crash!"

"The wall is collapsing," Danny said. "But slowly. Today the wall is a symbol of China. That was not always so. In the past century, people used the bricks for houses. Stones were taken to make dams and walls. People stored livestock in the towers."

"You mean they kept cows and goats and things in the watchtowers?" Grace asked.

When Danny nodded, Jaden said, "That's not as good as an explosion."

"You want excitement? In the desert, sands covered the wall. In the east, a reservoir flooded a valley to provide water for a city. Some parts of the wall are now under 100 feet of water. And in some places...." Danny grabbed Jaden and shook him playfully. "Earthquakes shook the wall!"

Jaden giggled.

"And there were explosions. During World War II, the Japanese bombed parts of the wall."

"Boom!" Jaden said.

"You know, many people died building the wall," Danny said. "People were afraid that the spirits of the dead would wander along the wall forever. When someone died, the family would put a white

rooster in a cage on top of the coffin. The rooster's crow was said to keep the dead person awake until he crossed the wall."

Grace didn't like to think of all the people who had died there. The wall had a sad history. It didn't look sad now, though. It was pretty and dramatic, the way it cut through the land. She wanted to think of China as a beautiful, peaceful place. But no place was perfect all the time. Sad and happy and scary and beautiful all got mixed together. Maybe it was good to know about the past. It made her glad she lived now. No one would make her build a huge wall to keep out enemies!

She turned to Danny. "Can you teach me some more Chinese?" She wanted to be able to talk to Joy when Mom and Dad brought her home. Plus, it would keep Danny from talking about dead people.

He agreed and they spent the morning practicing words and taking pictures. The wall was changing as they got farther from Beijing. It was no longer in such good condition. In some places, the wall had collapsed. They could see the rubble inside the wall's sides. Jaden looked carefully at the tumbled stones. He did not find a single bone!

They had lunch at a tower that was mostly ruined. The walls had collapsed and weeds grew between the stones. They each found a stone windowsill to sit on while they ate. It was nice to rest in the cool shade. They put on more sunscreen before starting to walk again.

The hiking became more difficult after lunch. Wherever there were stairs, the steps had crumbled. Weeds, bushes, and even small trees grew among the rocks. The parapets edging the wall had often crumbled so bricks lay in heaps. They no longer had side walls to keep them from falling over the edge.

"Be careful," Dad said. "It would be easy to get hurt here, and we're a long way from help. Plus, we don't want to hurt the wall by knocking off bricks. It's already falling apart, so let's not make it any worse!"

Grace watched where she put her feet. It wasn't much fun, since she couldn't see the scenery. But she didn't want to damage the wall – or herself!

Chapter Seven

Meeting a Mongol

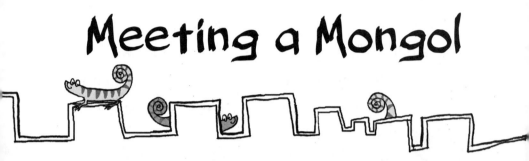

They walked carefully. The trees rustled in a light breeze, and sometimes a bird called. Grace's own footsteps sounded loud.

At another tower, a Chinese woman sat fanning herself. She jumped up when she saw them. "Hello, hello!" she called.

Danny nodded to her and kept walking. The woman smiled at Grace and said something in Chinese. Grace said "Nín hǎo," which means hello in Chinese, and the woman beamed. But when she chattered on in Chinese, Grace had to shake her head and say, "Sorry. I'm American."

The woman walked alongside her. She spoke English, though not as well as Danny. "I am Mongol," she said. "Mongol!" She tapped her chest and laughed.

Grace wasn't sure what that meant. She thought

Genghis Khan was a Mongol. He had invaded China. Was this woman claiming she was related to him?

The woman grabbed Grace's hand to help her up a steep slope. Grace did not really need help and she didn't like being touched by strangers, but she thought it would be rude to refuse. She glanced at her father and he smiled. Grace guessed he wasn't worried as long as he was close by.

When they reached the top of the slope, the woman pulled out a pretty paper fan and waved it at Grace. The cool air did feel nice. The woman started talking about her life. She had grown up on a farm, but the government made her move. They wanted to build a resort for rich tourists. She did not like her new apartment.

The woman asked Grace about her life. At first she assumed Danny was Grace's father. Grace explained that she had been adopted.

"Oh, that's why you no speak Chinese." The woman nodded rapidly. "You good girl. Very good."

She smiled at the woman and spoke slowly. "I'm happy to see China. It is very nice here." She hesitated, and then told the woman about Joy.

"I'm glad I get a sister. I hope she likes me."

"Your parents very lucky!" the woman said. "Three children. Big family is good fortune."

Sometimes Grace wished she were an only child. It sounded like she would have been if she'd stayed in China. What if her birth parents hadn't given her up for adoption? Would she have grown up on a farm? In the city? Would she know all about China, but nothing about America? Her life would have been very different. It was hard to imagine.

One thing she knew, she loved her parents. She liked her house, her school, and her friends. She loved Jaden, even if sometimes she didn't like him very much. She decided she would not worry about what might have happened. She would enjoy what she had.

After a while, the woman said goodbye. Dad gave her a little money. The woman held out the fan she had been using to fan Grace. When it was unfolded, the curved paper had a painting of pink flowers. Dad gave her a little more money and took the fan. He handed it to Grace and said, "A souvenir to help you remember this trip."

"Thank you." Grace let the woman hug her. She

even hugged back a little. The woman headed back the way she came.

Grace asked Danny, "Does she walk the wall every day? Why was she talking to me?"

"She was hoping to get a tip," he said. "The government moved many farmers off of their land. Some of them will work in tourism, but she probably does not have a job. She earns a little money as an unofficial guide."

That explained why Dad gave her money.

"She said she was a Mongol," Grace said.

Danny said, "People who live north of the wall sometimes call themselves Mongols. It is a joke. The Mongols once lived in that area."

"They were bad, right?"

Danny shrugged. "They were excellent horsemen. They lived to the west, on the plains. It gets very cold there. Sometimes the winter is so harsh that many animals die. With no livestock for food, the Mongols would try to invade China. They would take gold, livestock, and slaves."

Grace shuddered. "But the wall kept them out, right?"

"Sometimes. In truth, it was easy for a few men

to get over the wall. They killed many Chinese. But if they stole a lot of cows, how would they get them back to the other side? The wall kept the property in, more than it kept the enemy out."

"They could carry the cows on their backs!" Jaden said.

Dad chuckled. "I don't think so. A cow weighs over a thousand pounds – that's like five of me or almost twenty of you." Dad was scribbling in his notebook as he walked. His foot caught in a stone and he stumbled forward. His notebook and pencil went flying.

"Dad!" Grace exclaimed. He tottered on the edge of a steep slope. She grabbed for one of his swinging arms. For a moment she thought he was going to pull her off the wall.

Danny grabbed him as well. Dad sat down hard. "Oof! That was close." He pulled Grace closer, away from the edge.

Grace's voice shook a little as she said, "Now who needs to be careful?"

Dad grinned at her. "You are absolutely right. I should stop when I want to take notes."

Danny retrieved the notebook. "I'm not sure where the pencil went."

"I see it!" Jaden scrambled to the edge of the wall. It had crumbled here, leaving a slope filled with rocks.

"No!" Dad, Danny, and Grace all yelled at once. Grace was closest, so she grabbed for Jaden. She caught his arm just as he started to climb over the edge.

Jaden started squirming. "Let go!" His arm slipped out of Grace's grasp. He jerked away from her.

For a moment Grace saw Jaden's eyes go big. Then he started sliding over the edge.

Chapter Eight

Sounds in the Night

Grace grabbed for Jaden's leg. Her hands caught the fabric of his jeans as his head disappeared from sight.

He was heavy. Too heavy for her to hold. She was sliding toward the edge. But she couldn't let go or Jaden would roll all the way down the rocky slope. He'd be hurt for sure.

Arms closed around Grace, anchoring her in place. Danny scrambled past her on his knees. He reached over the edge and grabbed Jaden. A moment later, they were all sitting on flat ground, gasping for breath.

Jaden sniffled. "I wouldn't have fallen if you didn't knock me off balance."

Grace was too tired to argue.

Dad said, "You should not have gone so close to the edge in the first place." He held Jaden close and kissed the top of his head.

Danny wiped sweat from his forehead. "I like to tell stories about the scary things that happened here, but I do not want you to be one of those stories!"

"I know this part of the wall is called the wild wall," Dad said, "but I didn't realize how rough the path got. I must have been crazy to bring you kids on this hike."

"Maybe a little crazy," Danny agreed.

"No!" Grace said. "I'm glad we came. I've learned a lot. And I'm having fun. Mostly."

Dad held out an arm to her. Grace crawled over and nestled against him. He kissed the top of her head. "I'm glad for that." Dad sighed. "Maybe we're all just getting tired. How far to the tower where we'll spend the night?"

"Not far," Danny said. "We walk less today than yesterday." He got up and held out a hand to help the others. "While we walk, I will tell you a story." He gave Dad a stern look. "But you will not try to write it down while we walk!"

Dad chuckled. "Agreed."

"The wall was very expensive to maintain," Danny said as they picked their way across the rubble. "In the thirteenth century, the guards had not been paid for months. Winter was coming and they were running out of supplies. Then Genghis Khan came! He had fifty thousand Mongol warriors on horses. What do you think happened?"

"A huge battle!" Jaden said.

Danny shook his head. "No battle. He bribed the starving guards. They were hungry and poor, so instead of fighting, they let him pass. As Genghis Khan said, 'The strength of a wall depends on the courage of those who defend it.' The Mongols ruled China for almost a century, from 1279 to 1368. Another time someone opened a gate to let the enemy in. The wall did not really work."

Grace thought about that. "That's too bad. Other people shouldn't try to take over."

Dad said, "History is mostly about one group trying to take land from another."

"Yes," Danny said. "Another people, the Manchu, ruled China for two and a half centuries. And when the Europeans came by sea, the wall did not stop them."

"Wait," Grace said, "Europeans invaded too?"

"Yes, in the 1800s," Danny said. "There had been trade with Britain, Portugal, and the Dutch for many years. England wanted more trade. War broke out."

"The Opium War," Dad said.

Danny nodded. "Yes, the British were bringing drugs into China. They were very bad for the Chinese people. China wanted England to stop, but England did not want to lose the trade money." He shrugged. "There were many excuses, but really it was about trade. China was a great country at that time, but England had a stronger military. The wars ended in new treaties. These agreements were bad for China."

They came to a steep downslope. "Careful now, watch your step," Dad said.

Grace grinned. "You too," she said. They worked their way carefully down the slope.

When they reached flatter ground, Danny continued. "At the time of the wars, China also had problems inside the country. The population was growing too big, so there was not enough land to grow food for all the people. Then there were natural disasters: drought, famine, floods. The government was weak. People started to rebel. The last Chinese Emperor gave up the throne in 1912."

They paused to take drinks from their water bottles. Grace thought about what Danny was saying. She didn't understand all the politics, but she had heard about similar things at school. Today, the world still had natural disasters. Some countries had too many people and not enough land for food. And some people seemed to think making money was more important than being fair.

Grace looked at the wall stretching out for miles before them. "So all that work. All those people who died building the wall. It didn't do any good?"

"It helped sometimes," Danny said. "But in the end, no. Now China has a different way of defending its borders. Diplomacy."

"What's that?" Jaden asked. "Some kind of weapon?"

Danny laughed. "No, although the Chinese did invent rockets. But diplomacy means talking."

Jaden frowned. "That's boring."

"Diplomacy is very hard. You must listen carefully. You must be smart when you talk. You have to make the other side happy. At the same time, you want to be happy."

"How can you both be happy if you want different things?" Grace asked.

"You try to understand each other," Dad said. "And you compromise, so each side gives a little. You kids should try that more often. It beats fighting."

It was not easy to compromise with Jaden. He and Grace often liked very different things. But what about her new little sister? Would Grace have to compromise with Joy a lot?

They came to a watchtower. An open courtyard had walls with arched openings all around. In some places the walls were crumbling. Danny led them up a narrow staircase. The stairs were so steep that Grace used her hands, almost like climbing a ladder. Dad held onto Jaden.

"These towers are as tall as a three-story building," Dad said. "When they were built, they would have been the tallest buildings for miles and must have seemed like skyscrapers."

When they reached the top, Danny said, "Here the soldiers would have watched for the enemy. They could shoot arrows from the openings in the wall. They could also roll rocks down onto the enemy."

Jaden pretended to shoot arrows. "Why don't they use it now?"

Dad smiled. "I don't think China needs to defend its borders with bows and arrows anymore."

"There was fighting at the wall in the 1930s," Danny said. "When Japan invaded China, the wall held them back for a few days. Eventually the Japanese took control of all the important parts of the wall, though. You can still see the bullet holes in some places."

"The 1930s?" Dad frowned, and then nodded. "Oh, right, I forget that the Second World War started so much earlier here. The US didn't get involved until 1941."

"That was forever ago," Jaden said.

"There are a few people alive who still remember those days," Dad said.

"Do you?" Jaden asked.

Dad laughed. "I'm not that old!"

Jaden nodded. "Like I said, ancient history."

Danny chuckled and leaned toward Jaden. "I will tell you a secret. Part of the wall is still used today. It is at the edge of an army compound."

"Cool!" Jaden said. "What do they do there?"

"I don't know," Danny said. "They keep it secret, and they keep people out."

They heated up dinner on a camp stove. Everyone was too tired to talk much, but they practiced the Chinese Danny taught them.

After dinner, they spread out sleeping bags on the floor. "Just imagine!" Dad said. "Centuries ago, Chinese soldiers would have slept here. Maybe they heard the same sounds and smelled the same scents."

"Maybe they heard the same ghosts," Jaden said. "Lots of ghosts, from all those guys who died building the wall." He tried to sound spooky. "Whoooo!"

"There is no such thing as a ghost," Grace said.

Jaden leaned over her. "Whoooo!"

"That's enough, Jaden." Dad yawned. "Let's get some rest. Tomorrow we go back to Beijing."

The wind whistled as it blew through the window openings. A rustling came from outside. Grace told herself it was only the trees blowing in the wind. Something gray moved outside the window. Heart pounding, Grace sat up for a better look. It was only a quickly moving cloud that had seemed closer. She settled down and tried to sleep.

It wasn't easy. The ground was hard. Her legs were sore from all the walking. Her shoulders hurt from carrying the backpack. Someone started snoring. The wind rustled and howled. But she was so tired. She drifted off.

Grace woke in the night. She blinked, trying to figure out where she was. A strange gray light seemed to glow around her. Something scraped and rustled.

She remembered the Great Wall, and camping in the tower. The light was the moon shining on the gray stone. But what was that sound? Maybe someone got up.

Grace sat up and counted the bodies nearby: Dad, Jaden, Danny. No one was missing. The sound was coming from their pile of gear, about 15 feet away.

And then something moved.

Chapter Nine

Thieves!

Grace gasped. Was someone stealing their packs? What would the person do if he realized she was awake?

She sat frozen. The movement had stopped. Had they heard her gasp or seen her sit up? Was someone standing in the dark, watching her, waiting to see what she would do?

She was in the shadow cast by the wall. Surely no one could see her there. She had to wake the others. Jaden was curled up to one side of her. Dad was on the other side, but he had rolled away. She couldn't touch him without sliding over. Danny was on the other side of Jaden. If Grace could wake Jaden, they could each wake the grown-up beside them. Then she would feel safer.

Grace dropped her hand slowly. She slid her hand along the floor slowly, until she felt Jaden's hair. She worked her way down to his shoulder and squeezed. He let out a sigh.

A rustling came from near the packs. Was the thief coming toward her? She froze, waiting for a shape to loom out of the darkness. But the rustling stayed across the room. Had he been fooled by her silence?

Maybe it wasn't a person after all. Grace didn't want to make a sound. *There are no ghosts, there are no ghosts,* she thought over and over.

She squeezed Jaden's shoulder harder. "What?" he mumbled.

"Shh!" She eased down beside him to whisper in his ear. "Someone's over there."

Jaden went still. Together they listened to the rustling noises. Grace still couldn't see anyone near their packs. Maybe he was crouched down behind the pile.

Jaden sat up and stretched out his arm. From his hand, a flashlight beam speared through the night toward their packs. Grace had forgotten about the flashlight they placed between their sleeping bags.

The light bobbed around for a moment. Then it settled on a small brown creature standing on top of a backpack. It stared at them with eyes that glowed red in the flashlight beam. "A rat!" Jaden said.

The thing flipped around, showing off a long, fluffy tail. "No, a squirrel," Grace said. It wasn't quite like the squirrels back home, though. Whatever it was, the thing scrambled up to a window.

Grace and Jaden squirmed free of their sleeping bags and ran to the window. The creature leapt out into the air. "Oh!" Grace gasped. They were a couple of stories above the ground. But the little animal spread out its arms and legs. It became a square with a tail. It glided through the air and disappeared in the trees.

Behind them, Dad and Danny stirred. "What's wrong?" Dad asked.

Grace and Jaden explained what they saw, both trying to talk at the same time.

"Flying squirrel," Danny said. "It probably smelled our food."

Dad said, "I didn't even think about animals here. Back home, we would hang our packs from a tree branch to keep out the bears."

"Hard to keep packs away from a flying squirrel," Danny said. "They climb too well. But we have our food in sealed containers. You will not find many dangerous animals here. There are a few leopards in the mountains, but they are very shy. I have only seen one at the zoo."

Dad yawned. "Well, let's get back to sleep."

He and Danny settled down. Jaden went back to his sleeping bag. Grace stayed at the window, watching the moon rising in the sky. It shone on distant hills and mountains. The wall looked like a ghostly dragon's tail, softly glowing against the dark hills.

The moon was half full, so she could still see some stars. She picked out the Big Dipper. She could follow the two front stars of the dipper and find the North Star. She often did the same thing back home. Grace smiled in the darkness. In China, she could see the same stars as at home! It made the world seem smaller, in a good way.

Had Joy ever seen the Big Dipper? Probably not. She was only two years old. But when they were back home, Grace could take her mei mei out to see the stars. She would show her the Big Dipper. She could tell Joy that the Big Dipper shone over China, too. In a small way, it would connect them both to where they were born. Grace was Chinese and American. That was good. She could help Joy be both as well.

Grace went back to her sleeping bag. Hiking the wall had been fun, but she was looking forward to the end of the hike the next day. They would go back to Beijing and she would learn even more about China. In a week, they would go home. And in another month, Mom and Dad would come back to China to collect Joy. Grace couldn't wait. She was ready to be a jie jie – a big sister.

Grace's Travel Journal

In China, people have a different idea of personal space. They get a lot closer to you. They stand really close when waiting in lines. Buses get so crowded that people are crammed together. It's strange if you are used to America, where people mostly give you lots of room.

The Chinese drink a lot of tea, instead of coffee. But there are coffee shops, too—the same stores as in Seattle, Washington! They have many different types of tea. They also drink hot water and don't like cold water or ice water. While visiting, we could not drink water straight out of the faucet. It could make us sick, so we had to boil it first to kill the bacteria.

You can get Chinese food in America, but what you get in China is a little different. They eat most parts of the animal – skin, tails, and feet! Food is cut in small pieces when it's made, so you can eat with chopsticks. Everyone at the table shares all the dishes.

Country Facts

Capital: Beijing

Official Language: The official language is Standard Chinese, also called Mandarin. Many other languages are also spoken, including Cantonese.

Population: 1.3 billion, more than any other country.

Famous People: Confucius lived 2,500 years ago. He taught that it was important to love others. He wrote the Golden Rule: "Do not do to others that which we do not want them to do to us."

Mao Tse-tung was a military leader. He was important in politics from 1935 until 1962. He wanted to bring China into the modern world. He started a revolution called "The Great Leap Forward." He had some good ideas, but his methods were harsh and things didn't all work the way he wanted. His wife, Jiang Qing, was also important in politics.

Wu Zetian was China's first female Emperor. Her daughter-in-law, Shangguan Wan'er, was the first woman prime minister. They lived in the seventh century.

Events and Holidays

China has many holidays. New Year's Day is a big one. Schools hold parties! The Chinese follow a lunar, or moon-based, calendar. Each month starts when the moon is the darkest. This means the date of the New Year changes every year.

The Spring Festival also celebrates the New Year, but it lasts for two weeks. People want to get the New Year off to a good start. They clean the house and buy new clothes. They eat a lot of wonderful food. They try not to talk about bad things.

There are many other festivals. Each has its own special activities and foods. During one, people appreciate the stars. During another, they appreciate the moon. One is all about lanterns. During the Dragon Boat Festival, people race boats shaped like dragons.

China's Climate

China has many different climates because it is a large country—the fourth largest in the world. In the south, it is hot and humid. The north has short summers and very cold winters. The west has mountains and deserts. The east has plains, hills, and deltas where rivers flow into the sea. China includes Mount Everest, the highest point in Asia.

Landmarks

The Great Wall of China: A symbol of China. It's actually many different walls and forts. The earliest parts were built more than 2,000 years ago. The best-known parts were built from the 14th through 17th centuries. These are also the parts in the best condition.

The Forbidden City, Beijing: Not really a city, but a palace. It has more than 100 buildings, with nearly 10,000 rooms. There are also courtyards and beautiful gardens. It was the royal residence of the emperors from the 15th to 20th centuries. It was called "forbidden" because only the royal court and their servants could enter. It is no longer forbidden—the palace is now a museum you can visit.

Now and Then

The Great Wall of China is falling apart in places. Other parts of it have been rebuilt. Where it was rebuilt, it looks a lot like it did many years ago!

Now:

Discussion Questions:

1. Did you or your family members come from another country? How important are the cultural traditions of that country to you? Why?

2. Genghis Khan said, "The strength of a wall depends on the courage of those who defend it." What does this mean? Give an example of how it might apply today.

3. In chapter five, Danny shared a legend about the God of Thunder. Why might people make up stories to explain thunder or other natural events?

4. In China, many animals are associated with specific ideas. For example, crickets are a symbol of fighting spirit. Choose three of your favorite animals. What symbolism would you give them?

5. If you were lost in a strange place, what would you do?

6. Is it important to save historical sites such as the Great Wall? Why or why not?

7. The soldiers guarding the Great Wall sent signals with smoke, fire, and canons. How else could you send a message a short distance? What about a long distance?

Vocabulary

You can practice using these words by drawing a picture of the Great Wall. Label the different parts and the people and things on the wall. How many of these words can you use?

compromise	parallel
diplomacy	parapet
dynasty	peaked
eaves	picturesque
emperor	rubble
fortress	souvenir
landscape	symbolism
livestock	tourists
martial arts	watchtower
mortar	Westerners

Websites to Visit

http://kids.nationalgeographic.com/explore/countries/china
www.timeforkids.com/destination/china
www.atozkidsstuff.com/china.html

About the Author

M. M. Eboch writes fiction and nonfiction for all ages. Writing as Chris Eboch, her novels for young people include *The Genie's Gift*, a middle eastern fantasy; *The Eyes of Pharaoh*, a mystery in ancient Egypt; and the Haunted series, which starts with *The Ghost on the Stairs*. As M. M. Eboch, her books include nonfiction and the fictionalized biographies *Jesse Owens: Young Record Breaker* and *Milton Hershey: Young Chocolatier*. Visit her at www.chriseboch.com.

About the Illustrator

Sarah Horne studied illustration at Falmouth College of Arts, England, graduating in 2001. Sarah now specializes in funny inky illustration and text for young fiction and picture books. She also works on book covers, magazine and newspaper editorials and in Advertising. She loves music, painting, color, photography, film, scratchy jazz and a good cup of coffee.

Sarah lives on a hill in London, UK.